Treasured Tales

Beauty and the Beast

p

Once upon a time there was a man who lived in a cottage in the country with his three daughters. His youngest daughter was so pretty that everyone called her "Beauty," which made her two sisters very angry and jealous.

One day the man had to go to the city. Before he left, he told his daughters that he would bring each of them a present, and he asked what they would like.

"Jewels!" the eldest daughter demanded. "Silk dresses!" said the second daughter. But all Beauty asked for was a single white rose.

On his way home, the father was caught in a snowstorm and lost his way. The blizzard was so thick and fierce and the forest so large and dark that he nearly gave up hope of ever finding his home. Then, through the mist, he glimpsed a grand palace.

He staggered to the great door — there seemed to be no one about. Inside, he found a table set with a magnificent dinner. The man ate hungrily, then searched the house. Upstairs, he found a huge bed, where he gratefully fell into an exhausted sleep. In the morning, when he awoke, breakfast was waiting beside the bed.

As he set off on his way home the man noticed a wonderful rose garden. Remembering Beauty's request, he stopped to pick a white rose. Suddenly, with a mighty roar, a terrifying, snarling Beast appeared.

"I have welcomed you with every comfort," he growled, "and in return you steal my roses!"

Shaking with fear, the man begged for forgiveness. "I only wanted the rose as a present for my daughter!"

"I will spare you," said the Beast, "but only if your daughter comes to live here of her own free will. If not, you must return in three months."

Back home, the man tearfully told his daughters what had happened. To his surprise, Beauty agreed to go.

When she arrived at the palace, a glorious meal was waiting for her. "The Beast must want to fatten me up," she thought. But she sat and ate.

As soon as Beauty finished her meal, the Beast appeared. He was truly horrifying, and she was frightened.

"Your room is all ready," said the Beast, and he led her to a door that said "Beauty's Room" in gold letters.

The room was everything Beauty could have wished for. She saw a little piano, beautiful silk dresses, and fresh, fragrant roses. On the dressing table was a mirror with these words on it:

If anything you long to see,
Speak your wish, and look in me.

"I wish I could see my father," said Beauty, and instantly she saw her father in the mirror, sitting sadly beside the fire at home.

"Perhaps the Beast doesn't mean to kill me after all," Beauty thought. "I wonder what he does want?"

The next evening the Beast joined Beauty for supper. "Tell me," he said, "am I truly horrible to look at?"

Beauty could not lie. "You are," she said. "But I know that you are very kind-hearted."

"Then," said the Beast, "will you marry me?"

Beauty was surprised. She knew he might be angry if she refused, but she couldn't say yes if she didn't love him. "No," she said. "I will not marry you."

The Beast sighed so heavily that the walls shook. "Good night, then," he said sadly. And he left her to finish her supper alone.

Months passed, and the Beast gave Beauty everything she could want. She was very happy in the palace.

Every evening, the Beast asked the same question: "Will you marry me?" And Beauty always said no. But she was growing very fond of him.

One day, Beauty looked in the magic mirror and saw that her father was very ill. She begged the Beast to let her go home, and sadly he agreed.

"Take this magic ring," he told her. "If you ever want to come back, put it by your bedside, and when you wake up, you will be here."

"I will come back," Beauty promised.

So Beauty went home to look after her father. He was soon well again, and she was ready to go back to the Beast. But her jealous sisters hated to think of Beauty going back to a palace while they still lived in a small cottage. So they convinced her to stay a while longer.

One night, Beauty dreamed that the Beast was lying dead in his garden, and she woke up in tears. She knew then that she loved the Beast, and had to return to him.

Putting the magic ring by her bedside, Beauty lay down again and closed her eyes.

When she opened them again, Beauty was back in the Beast's garden — and, true to her dream, he was lying lifeless on the ground.

"Oh, Beast," she cried, taking him in her arms, "please don't die! I love you, and I want to marry you!"

All at once light and music filled the air, and the Beast vanished. In his place stood a handsome prince.

"Who are you?" cried Beauty.

"I was your Beast," said the prince. "An evil witch cast a spell on me and turned me into that poor animal. The spell could only be broken when a beautiful girl agreed to marry me."

A few days later they were married, and Beauty's family came to join in the joyous celebrations at the palace.

Beauty had never been so happy. She loved the prince with all her heart, and they lived in their rose palace happily ever after.